Christmas Tree

David Martin

illustrated by Melissa Sweet

CANDLEWICK PRESS

Tree

Bird

Bird in the tree

Mouse

Mouse in the tree

Squirrel

Squirrel in the tree

Rabbit

Rabbit in the tree

Ball

Ball in the tree

Snowflake in the tree

Sled

Sled in the tree

Stars

Star in the tree

House

Tree in the house

Pretty tree,
Sparkling bright.
Christmas Eve—
Is it tonight?

First paperback sticker edition 2015

Library of Congress Catalog Card Number 2009920349
ISBN 978-0-7636-3030-0 (board book)
ISBN 978-0-7636-7968-2 (paperback with stickers)

15 16 17 18 19 20 APS 10 9 8 7 6 5 4 3 2 1

Printed in Humen, Dongguan, China

This book was typeset in Avril.
The illustrations were done in watercolor and collage.

Candlewick Press
99 Dover Street
Somerville, Massachusetts 02144

visit us as www.candlewick.com